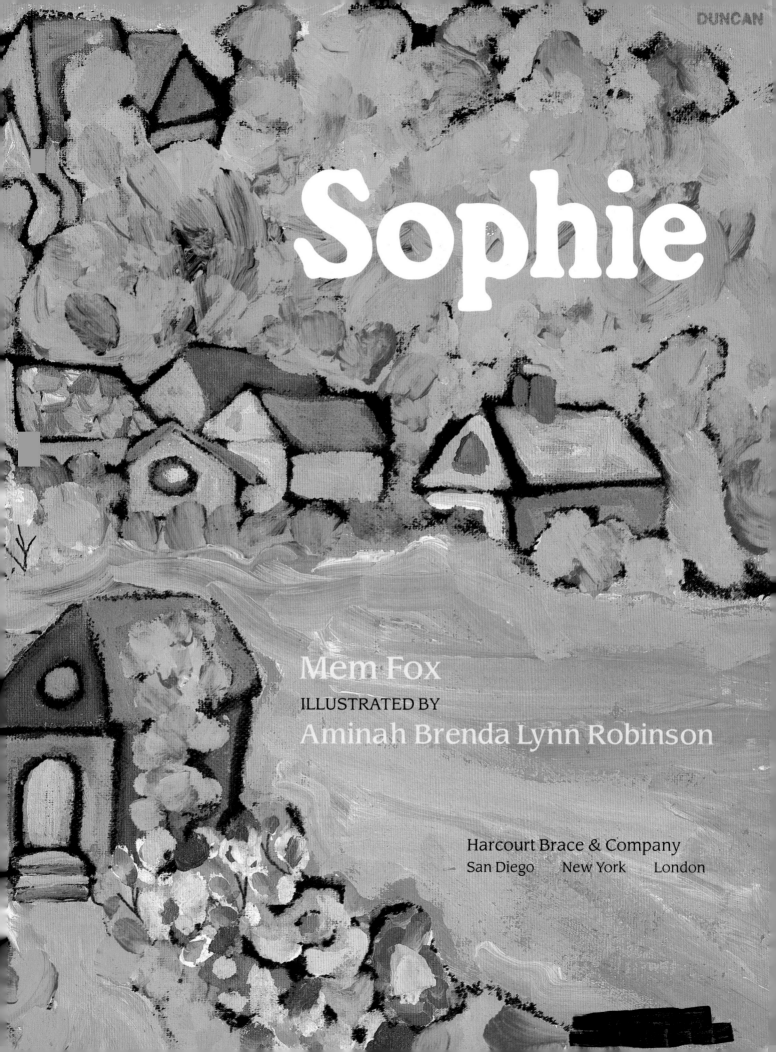

Sophie

Mem Fox

ILLUSTRATED BY

Aminah Brenda Lynn Robinson

Harcourt Brace & Company

San Diego   New York   London

Text copyright © 1994, 1989 by Mem Fox
Illustrations copyright © 1994 by
Aminah Brenda Lynn Robinson

First published 1989 by
Ian Drakeford Publishing Pty Ltd, Australia

Library of Congress Cataloging-in-Publication Data
Fox, Mem, 1946–
Sophie/written by Mem Fox; illustrated by Aminah Brenda
Lynn Robinson. — 1st ed.
p.   cm.
Summary: As Sophie grows bigger and her grandfather gets
smaller, they continue to love each other very much.
ISBN 0-15-277160-3
[1. Grandfathers — Fiction. 2. Death — Fiction. 3. Birth—Fiction.]
I. Robinson, Aminah Brenda Lynn, ill. II. Title.
PZ7.F8373So   1994
[E] — dc20   94-1976

First edition
A B C D E

The paintings in this book were done in acrylics, dyes, and
house paint on rag cloth.
The display type was set in Gorilla and the text type was set
in Leawood Book by Thompson Type, San Diego, California.
Color separations were made by Bright Arts, Ltd., Singapore.
This book was printed with soya-based inks on Leykam recycled
paper, which contains more than 20 percent postconsumer waste
and has a total recycled content of at least 50 percent.
Printed and bound by Tien Wah Press, Singapore
Production supervision by Warren Wallerstein and David Hough
Designed by Lydia D'moch

Printed in Singapore

For Frank Hodge
        —M. F.

In memory of my father
        —A. B. L. R.

Once there was no Sophie.

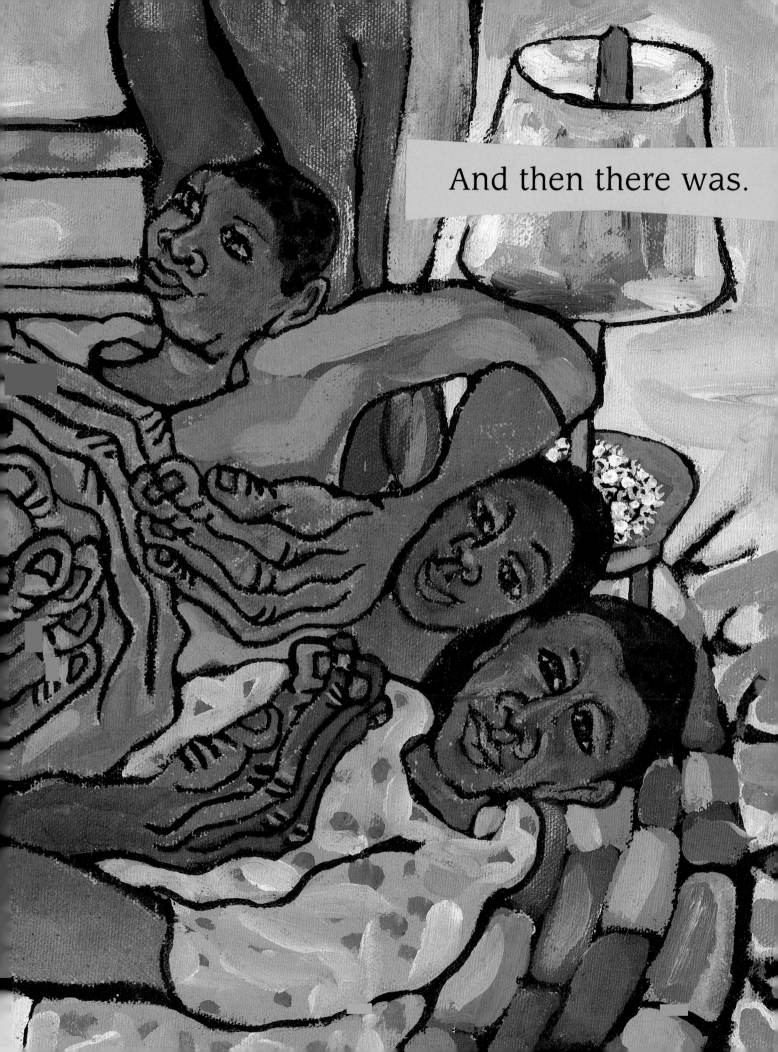

And then there was.

Sophie's hand curled round Grandpa's finger.

Grandpa and little Sophie loved each other.

Sophie grew

and grew

and grew

till she was big enough

to work with Grandpa,

big enough to look Grandpa in the eye.

Grandpa grew older

and slower

and smaller.

Sophie and little Grandpa loved each other.

Grandpa's hand held on to Sophie's.

And then there was no Grandpa,

just emptiness and sadness for a while,

till a tiny hand held
on to Sophie's

and sweetness filled the world, once again.